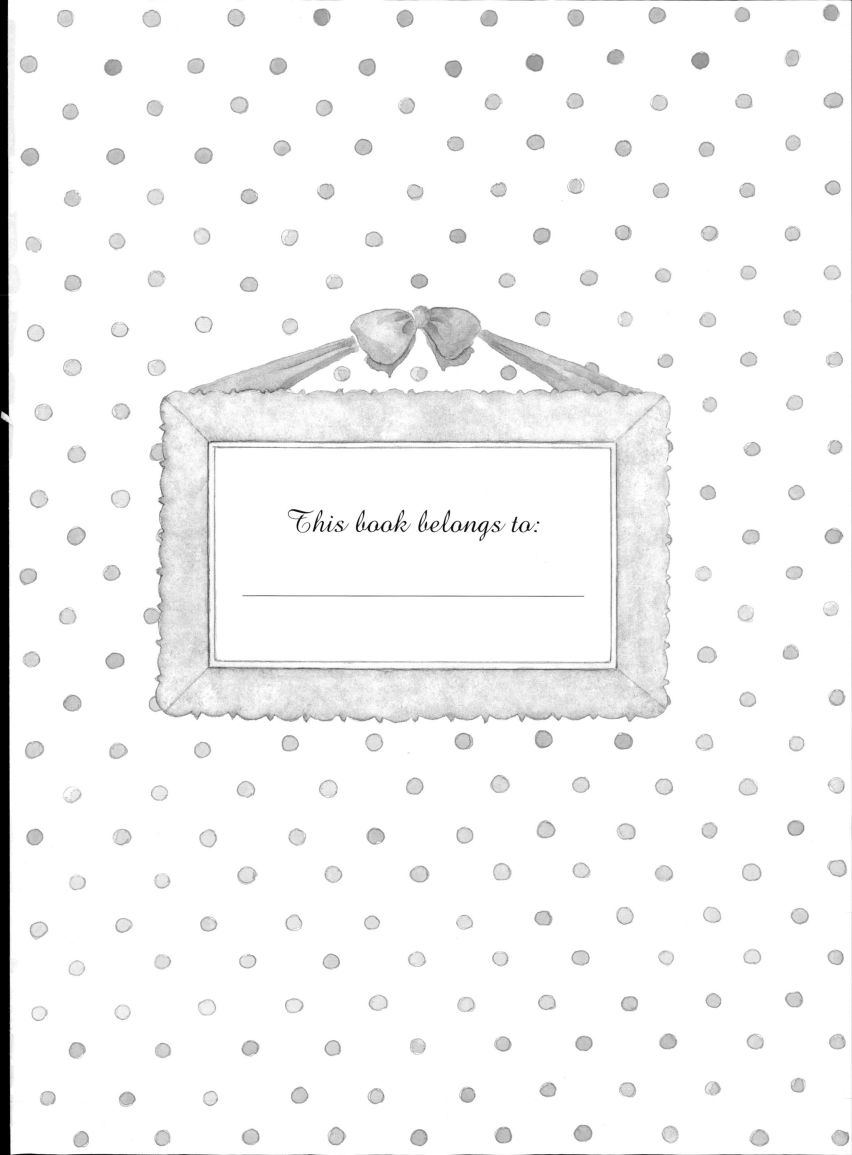

This book belongs to:

_____

Good Morning, Sweetie Pie

And Other Poems for Little Children

CYNTHIA RYLANT

Illustrated by JANE DYER

Simon & Schuster Books for Young Readers

New York   London   Toronto   Sydney   Singapore

SIMON & SCHUSTER BOOKS FOR YOUNG READERS

An imprint of Simon & Schuster Children's Publishing Division

1230 Avenue of the Americas New York, New York 10020

Text copyright © 2001 by Cynthia Rylant

Illustrations copyright © 2001 by Jane Dyer

SIMON & SCHUSTER BOOKS FOR YOUNG READERS

is a trademark of Simon & Schuster.

Book design by Jane Dyer and Paul Zakris

The text of this book is set in 18-point Berkeley Oldstyle.

The illustrations are rendered in Winsor and Newton

watercolors on Waterford 140-pound hot press paper.

Printed in Hong Kong

2 4 6 8 10 9 7 5 3 1

LIBRARY OF CONGRESS CATALOGING-IN-PUBLICATION DATA

Rylant, Cynthia

Good morning, sweetie pie, and other poems for little children

/ by Cynthia Rylant ; illustrated by Jane Dyer.

p. cm.

ISBN 0-689-82377-0

1. Family—Juvenile poetry. 2. Children's poetry, American.

[1. Parent and child—Poetry. 2. Babies—Poetry.

3. American poetry.] I. Dyer, Jane, ill. II. Title.

PS3568.Y55 G66 2002

811'.54—dc21

00-058785

*Jane Dyer would like to thank the people at
Smith College Child Care Center at Sunnyside for their assistance.*

Contents

Good Morning, Sweetie Pie

Baby Has a Sandbox

Little Cutie-Face

Baby Loves a Rainy Day

Going in the Car

Baby Has a Bath Today

Sweetie's Messes

Sleepy-boy

Good Morning, Sweetie Pie

When the birds begin their singing
and the sun begins its sunning
and the morning glories
open up all blue . . .
there's a mama or a papa
or a gramma somewhere saying:
"Good morning, Sweetie Pie,
how are you?"

And a child is slowly waking,
slowly taking his sweet time,
he's been flying in his dreams
the whole night through.
But his little ears hear someone
and he knows it's someone dear
who is saying: "'Morning, Honey,
I love you."

There's a kiss upon a finger
and another on a nose
and a tickle on some tiny baby feet.
There's a wiggle under covers
and a giggle in the dark
and an "Oh, Cutie Dumpling, you're so sweet!"

And a child is peeking out now
on this warm and yellow day,
he is peeking at the dear one by his bed.
It is Mama or it's Papa,
maybe Gramma come to visit,
saying, "Where's that little Apple Sleepyhead?"

And the sleepyhead is up now,
he is rubbing sleepy eyes,
he is yawning big and stretching out his toes.
And his mama or his papa
or his gramma-come-to-visit
tells him, "Let's get us some crunchy Oaty-O's!"

So the child comes into morning
where the birds are gently singing
and the glories are still
blooming in the sun.
And he sits up at the table
with his dear one right beside him
who is saying:
"'Morning, Angel, you're my One."

And then Sweetie eats his breakfast
while the dear one calls him "Sugar"
and a puppy licks
his little baby toes.
It is morning in the kitchen
and there's nothing could be better
than a dear one
and some crunchy Oaty-O's!

Baby Has a Sandbox

Baby has a sandbox,
he fills it up with trucks.
He adds a few long-neck giraffes
and little baby ducks.
He sprinkles in some little men
and little women, too.
Then stirs them with a little stick
to make a sandbox goo.
Baby plays there until ten
and then it's time to nap.
He carries everybody in—
poor Mama's sandy lap!
But Mama doesn't mind at all
her sandy baby's toys.
'Cause Mama knows that life is best
with sandy baby boys!

Little Cutie-Face

Papa loves to give a ride
to little Cutie-Face.
He picks her up and gallops off
and takes her place to place.
He takes his Cutie up the hill
and gallops her back down.
He rides her to the castle
and around the castle-town.
He takes her to the ocean
on his bumpy papa-back,
then stands right in the middle
with his little Cutie-pack!
Papa and his Cutie-Face
go riding here and there,
and there is so much silliness
that neighbors stop and stare.

Then when the ride is over
Papa gallops in the house,
and sneaks two cookies and some milk
to his small Cutie-mouse.
Papa loves to give a ride,
it brightens up his day
to take his little Cutie-girl
upon his back and play.
And Cutie loves her papa so,
he's such a funny horse!
Of all the papas in the world,
she thinks he's best, of course!

Baby Loves a Rainy Day

Baby loves a rainy day,
his mama keeps him in to play.
She brings out all his baby toys
(the special ones for baby boys).
He puts some people in a house
and reads a book about a mouse.
He rolls a ball across the room
and sweeps the carpet with a broom.
He stacks some toy blocks up high
and cuts a piece of dough-y pie.
Then Mama puts some music on
and Baby sings a baby-song.
Baby loves a rainy day
when Mama keeps him in to play.

Going in the Car

Going in the car today
going into town,
little Girl and Papa
with the windows halfway down.
Waving to the paperboy,
waving to the train,
waving to the kitty cat,
waving to the plane.
Papa plays the radio
and sings a Papa song.
Little Girl and Mrs. Bear,
they always sing along.
Stopping at the grocery store,
stopping for the mail,
stopping at the hardware now,
'cause Papa needs a nail.

Going in the car today
going into town.
Little Girl and Papa
with the windows halfway down.

Baby Has a Bath Today

Baby has a bath today,
he takes his teddy bear.
He fills his hands with baby soap
and washes Teddy's hair.
His mama washes Baby's ears
and Baby's pretty neck.
She rubs a cloth on Baby's legs
and gives his toes a check.
When Baby and his teddy
are all bright and squeaky clean,
Mama dries them off and then
they eat a tangerine.

Sweetie's Messes

At suppertime when Sweetie eats
She surely makes a mess,
With carrots in her curly hair
And green beans on her dress.
Papa tries to keep her clean
But he's no help at all,
His hair is full of apples
And a meatball's down the hall.
The puppy loves when Sweetie eats,
He licks up her spaghetti.
If Sweetie drops a tasty noodle,
Puppy's always ready!
Suppertime with baby girl
Leaves Papa looking funny.
He's got some squash in his left ear
And one shoe's full of honey!
But Papa loves this baby so,
He doesn't mind her messes.
He'll just keep washing Sweetie's face
And washing Sweetie's dresses!

Sleepy-boy

"Time for bed,"
says Mama-dear,
who picks up Sleepy-boy.
She finds his favorite blanket
and his favorite
sleeping toy.
She puts him
in his jammies
and she carries him to bed.
Then covers him
with little stars
and kisses his sweet head.
She turns his little
moon-light on
and lines up every bear.
She puts the horse
and donkey in
the stable that they share.
Now animals and boys
can sleep safe the whole night through.
'Cause Mama's watching over them . . .
that's what mamas do.

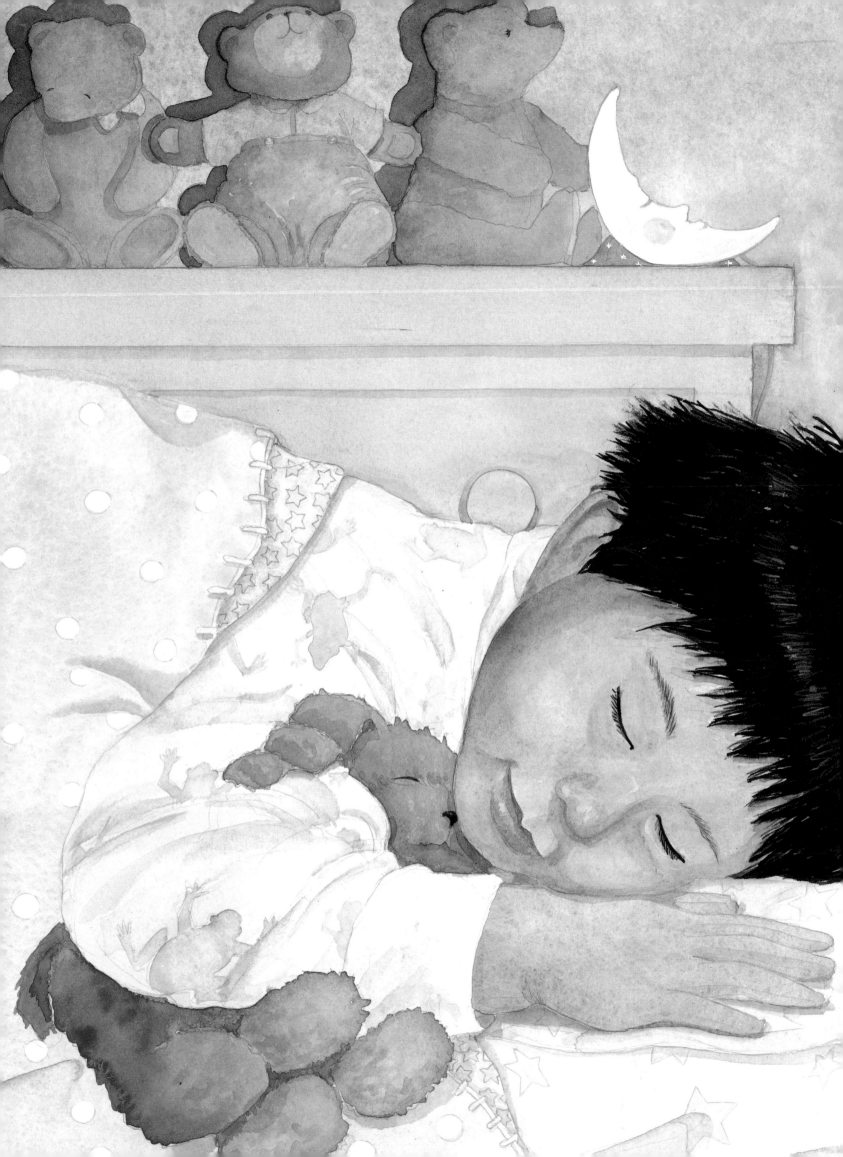

Special Thanks to These Sweetie Pies

MINH

Contents

LEON

Good Morning, Sweetie Pie

EZRA

Baby Has a Sandbox

AURORA

Little Cutie-Face

AMAL

Baby Loves a Rainy Day

AISHA

Going in the Car

WILLY

Baby Has a Bath Today

ISABELLA

Sweetie's Messes

ALEX

Sleepy-boy